"HELLO READING books are a perfect introduction to reading. Brief sentences full of word repetition and full-color pictures stress visual clues to help a child take the first important steps toward reading. Mastering these story books will build children's reading confidence and give them the enthusiasm to stand on their own in the world of words."

—Bee Cullinan
Past President of the International Reading
Association, Professor in New York University's
Early Childhood and Elementary Education Program

"Readers aren't born, they're made. Desire is planted—planted by parents who work at it."

—Jim Trelease
author of *The Read Aloud Handbook*

"When I was a classroom reading teacher, I recognized the importance of good stories in making children understand that reading is more than just recognizing words. I saw that children who have ready access to story books get excited about reading. They also make noticeably greater gains in reading comprehension. The development of the HELLO READING stories grows out of this experience."

—Harriet Ziefert
M.A.T., New York University School of Education
Author, Language Arts Module,
Scholastic Early Childhood Program

For Jon and Jamie

PUFFIN BOOKS
Published by the Penguin Group
Viking Penguin Inc., 40 West 23rd Street, New York, New York 10010, U.S.A.
Penguin Books Ltd, 27 Wrights Lane, London W8 5TZ, England
Penguin Books Australia Ltd, Ringwood, Victoria, Australia
Penguin Books Canada Ltd, 2801 John Street, Markham, Ontario, Canada L3R 1B4
Penguin Books (N.Z.) Ltd, 182-190 Wairau Road, Auckland 10, New Zealand

Penguin Books Ltd, Registered Offices: Harmondsworth, Middlesex, England

First published in Puffin Books, 1989 • Published simultaneously in Canada

1 3 5 7 9 10 8 6 4 2

Printed in Singapore for Harriet Ziefert, Inc.

HOW BIG IS BIG?

Harriet Ziefert
Pictures by Andrea Baruffi

PUFFIN BOOKS

What's big?
Look and see.

This elephant is big—
bigger than a man.
But...

Have you ever seen
a baby elephant?

This man is big—
bigger than a baby elephant.

What's small?
Look and see.
This dog is small—

smaller than a lady.
But...

Have you ever seen a Great Dane?

This man is small—
smaller than a Great Dane.

What's bigger than an elephant?

Dinosaurs are bigger.

Whales are bigger
than elephants.

Airplanes are bigger
than whales and elephants.

Skyscrapers are bigger
than airplanes and
whales and elephants.

What's smaller than a dog?

Rabbits are smaller
than dogs.

Mice are smaller
than rabbits and dogs.

Most bugs are smaller
than mice and
rabbits and dogs.

Many things are smaller
than the smallest bugs.

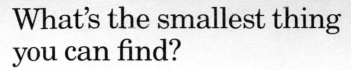

What's the smallest thing
you can find?

Many things are bigger
than the biggest skyscraper.

What's the biggest thing you can find?

A star?

The moon?

A planet?

The universe?

How big are you?
How small are you?